JUDITH CASELEY

We're the fastest!

We're the best!

Field
Day
Friday

GREENWILLOW BOOKS • *An Imprint of HarperCollinsPublishers*

Watercolor paints, colored pencils, and a black pen were used for the full-color art.
The text type is Souvenir Medium.

Field Day Friday
Copyright © 2000 by Judith Caseley
Printed in Hong Kong by South China Printing Company (1988) Ltd.
All rights reserved. http://www.harperchildrens.com

Library of Congress Cataloging-in-Publication Data
Caseley, Judith.
Field Day Friday / by Judith Caseley.
p. cm.
"Greenwillow Books."
Summary: On field day, Mickey is upset when he loses a race to his best friend Longjohn.
ISBN 0-688-16761-6 (trade). ISBN 0-688-16762-4 (lib. bdg.)
[1. Racing—Fiction. 2. Best friends—Fiction.] I. Title.
PZ7.C2677Fi 2000
[E]—dc21 98-45381 CIP AC

1 2 3 4 5 6 7 8 9 10 First Edition

For Michael and Jenna
and their winning
ways...

Mickey's best friend lived right next door.
His name was John, but everyone called him Longjohn.

NEWBORN IDENTIFICATION

INFANT – Name			Hospital No.
John Sidoti			

Infant's Birth Date	Time	Sex
9/14/	5⁴⁷/A	BOY

	Weight	Length
	10 lbs 002	22"

INFANT'S LEFT FOOTPRINT (or palmprint) INFANT'S RIGHT FOOTPRINT (or palmprint)

Physician	Delivery Room Nurse	Nursery Nurse
DSWS	Mary Darby RN	

When John was born, the nurse remarked, "This baby's so long, he's off the chart!"
She called him Longjohn, and the nickname stuck.

Mickey and Longjohn did everything together.
In the morning they went outside in their pajamas.
Mickey got the newspaper, and Longjohn decided
what the weather would be like.

They put on their knapsacks
and walked to school together.
Mama and Jenna trailed behind.
"Big and little," said Jenna to Mama.
"What a riot," said Mama.

Mickey and Longjohn played together every day after school.
Sometimes they collected bugs at Longjohn's house, with
their nets and their jars.
When Jenna went with them, she set the bugs free.

Sometimes they made a tent at Mickey's house, using sheets and pillows and chairs and tables.

If Mama wasn't looking, they shared snacks underneath.

Sometimes they ran.

Mickey was short and sturdy and quick.

Longjohn was tall and thin and speedy.

When they raced in the playground, it was often a tie.

"You're fast!" said Mickey.

"So are you!" said Longjohn.

When Mickey announced that
it was Field Day on Friday,
Mama said, "How wonderful!"
Papa said, "You'll enjoy the games."
Jenna said, "Maybe you'll win a prize."

Field Day arrived, and the children were divided into
teams of different colors.
Mickey and Longjohn were on the Blue Team together.
"My favorite color," said Mickey.
"Mine, too," said Longjohn. "It will give us good luck."

Mama and Papa and Jenna
came to watch.
The games began.

"Egg and Spoon," announced
the gym teacher, handing Mickey
a spoon with an egg on it.
Mickey walked slowly
and handed it to Jessica.
Jessica took baby steps
and handed it to Longjohn,
who took the spoon carefully
but dropped the egg quickly.
"Now all we need is bacon,"
said Mickey, which made
Longjohn laugh.

It was time for the Crabwalk.

Jeffrey scuttled backward on his hands and his feet.

Then came Amanda, who bumped into Mickey,

who nearly landed on Longjohn. The Blue Team won.

"Crabs like blue," explained Mickey.

"It reminds them of water," said Longjohn.

The next game they played was
called Waiter and Waitress.
Longjohn took a tray,
laid a napkin on top,
then a cup and a saucer,
a spoon, and a fork.
He was ready to go.
He held the tray like a waiter
with his hand in the air
and carried it to Hayley,
who carried the tray as it rattled and shook and
handed it to Mickey. Mickey started walking,
but the napkin flew away and got caught in a tree.
"The tree was hungry," said Longjohn when the Blue Team
lost, which made Mickey laugh.

It was time for Dress-Up Race.

Troy put on a big shirt and a huge pair of trousers and an oversized hat and some enormous boots. Then he tramped over to Jessica and took off the clothing, and Jessica got dressed and stomped over to Mickey, who stuck his head through an armhole.

"I need practice," said Mickey, handing the bundle to Longjohn.

"My mother helps me," said Longjohn when the pants gave him trouble.

The Orange Team won.

"Maybe their mothers don't help them," whispered Mickey to Longjohn.

"Maybe not," said Longjohn.

"Shoe Race!" cried the gym teacher.

The children unlaced their sneakers and threw them into a heap.

When a whistle blew, everyone dove into the pile to find their

shoes again, but Mickey's left sneaker was buried at the bottom.

He was slow putting it on, and the Yellow Team won.

"Their shoes had more Velcro," said Longjohn to Mickey.

The gym teacher announced the Fifty-Yard Dash.

"We're the best," said Longjohn.

"We're the fastest," said Mickey.

"Don't brag," said Mama.

"Tie your sneakers," said Papa.

"Win a medal," said Jenna.

"On your mark, get set, go!"
cried the gym teacher.
The children started running
and running and running,
and Mickey pulled ahead.
Then Longjohn caught up
and passed Mickey by a foot.
Then Mickey sprinted forward,
and they were neck and neck.
He was close to the finish line,
and he knew he was winning.

And then his sneaker fell off.

Mickey put it back on, but it fell off again, and the children kept running, and Longjohn won a ribbon that said, "First Place Runner."

The children started laughing
when Mickey crossed the finish line
with his sneaker in his hand.
"It's not funny," said Jenna.
"What a shame," said Mama.
"I should have tied his shoelaces," said Papa.
"They laughed," said Mickey,
"and I came in last."

It was time for watermelon, and everybody ate some,
except for Mickey, who said he wasn't hungry.
Then they all went home.

Mickey stayed inside for the longest time.

When Longjohn came over, Mickey wouldn't make a tent
or hunt for bugs or go to the playground.

"He's upset," said Jenna, but she had an idea.

Jenna took Longjohn to the kitchen, found her glue and
her glitter, her marker and some cloth, and they set to work.
When they were finished, Jenna called Mickey.
Longjohn said, "And now for your prize . . ."
He and Jenna took a ribbon made of cloth, glue, and glitter,
and they pinned it on Mickey.
On the front, Jenna had written, "First Place Brother."
Underneath, Longjohn wrote, "First Place Friend."

"It's nice," said Mickey. "But I wish it was for running."

"Next year," said Jenna.

"We'll come in together," said Longjohn.

"They'll have to give us two medals," said Mickey,
and he started to smile.

Then they all went bug-hunting,
and when they were finished,

Jenna set the bugs free.